A Very Merry Unauthorized Children's Scientology Pageant

Book, Music and Lyrics by
Kyle Jarrow

From a concept by
Alex Timbers

A SAMUEL FRENCH ACTING EDITION

SAMUEL FRENCH

FOUNDED 1830

NEW YORK HOLLYWOOD LONDON TORONTO

SAMUELFRENCH.COM

MUSIC USE NOTE

A VERY MERRY UNAUTHORIZED CHILDREN'S SCIENTOLOGY PAG-EANT was originally presented by Les Freres Corbusier at The Tank and The John Houseman Theatre, New York, NY, November-January, 2004, Aaron Lemon-Strauss, Producer. The Production Designer was Jenn Rogien with Scenic Design by David Evans Morris, and Lighting Design by Juliet Chia. The Stage Manager was Bailie Slevin. The production was under the direction of Alex Timbers assisted by David Kilpatrick with the following cast members: Seamus Boyle, Spenser Lee Carrion-O'Driscoll, Alison Stacy Klein, Joshua Marmer, Max Miner, Stephanie Favoreto Queiroz, Daren Watson, Emma Whitfield, Sophie Whitfield, and Jordan Wolfe.

:

AUTHOR'S NOTES

The play is intended to be performed by a cast of children, ideally ages 8-13. With doubling, a cast of seven or eight children is sufficient, but the more the merrier.

The show should only be performed by children, not by adults pretending to be children. This isn't *You're a Good Man Charlie Brown*!

In the original production, the songs were performed karaoke-style against pre-recorded CD playback of arrangements that combined the space-age feel of Scientology with a kiddie-rock spirit. The vocal track on the song "Rain" (on Page 32-34) was pre-recorded over the existing instrumental track by the actor playing L Ron, and lip-synched by the actress playing Annie. At the end of the play (Page 37), the eerie sounds of looping childrens' voices were pre-recorded and played as the actors stared blankly at the audience.

Alternatively, a live pianist can accompany the songs. In this scenario, the vocals on "Rain" could be sung live by L Ron from offstage and lip-synched by the actress playing Annie. The eerie sounds of childrens' voices at the end of the play could be sung live, a capella and expressionless.

The final sequence is described in the script as it was performed in the original production. This sequence required fly space and significant technical capabilities, which are obviously not options for all productions. Directors are encouraged to create their own unique sequence for the end of the play. Whatever they do, it should explode the space in a shocking and theatrical way—and it should reinforce the eerie sensation of the children being emptied of emotion and individuality.

The quote from L Ron Hubbard on Page 7 was taken from his book *Scientology: A New Slant on Life* (Bridge Publications: 1989).

Special thanks to The Fabulous Entourage, Steve Saporito, George Lane, Corinne Hayoun, Jason Cooper, Peter Franklin, Jonathan Lomma, Anne Tanaka, Eric Krebs, Mikey Greenberg, Reed Ridgley, Rebecca Habel, Alex Timbers, Aaron Lemon-Strauss, Sarah Sloboda, Rob Giampietro, my family, the original cast and their very understanding and supportive families. —K.J.

Scene 1

"Opening"

(In the dark, the sound of sleighbells, soft and rhythmic. A soft wintery light illuminates the ANGELIC GIRL. She wears angel wings and a halo. She sings.)

ANGELIC GIRL.
THE SNOW IS FALLING
ON THIS HOLY WINTER NIGHT
SLEIGHBELLS ARE RINGING
BUT NOTHING FEELS RIGHT.

(Spotlight up on another child: the boy who will later play L RON.)

L RON. "You remember when you were maybe five years old, and you went out in the morning and you looked at the day, and it was a very, very beautiful day, and you looked at the flowers and they were *very* beautiful flowers. Twenty-five years later you get up in the morning, you take a look at the flowers—they are wilted. The day isn't a happy day. Well, what has changed? You know they are the same flowers, it's the same world, something must have changed. Probably, it was you."
ANGELIC GIRL. L Ron Hubbard.

(Two more children ENTER and join L RON and the ANGELIC GIRL in song.)

L RON, ANGELIC GIRL & TWO OTHERS.
THE SNOW IS FALLING
AND THE FLOWERS ALL ARE DEAD
BUT DON'T GIVE UP YET
IT'S ALL INSIDE YOUR HEAD.

*(The music picks up in tempo. The lights come up and the rest of the
children ENTER. They all wear robes. They join the ANGELIC
GIRL, L RON, and the others, and they all sing jubilantly.)*

   ALL.
IT'S TIME TO CELEBRATE
TIME TO OPEN UP YOUR EYES
IT'S TIME TO RAISE YOUR VOICE
TIME TO SING IT TO THE SKIES
IT'S A HAPPY DAY
AND THE FLOWERS ARE IN BLOOM
IF YOU ARE NOT OKAY
WE KNOW YOU WILL BE SOON.

(A SOLOIST steps forward and sings.)

   SOLOIST.
THERE ARE PEOPLE HURTING
PEOPLE JUST LIKE YOU
THEY KNOW SOMETHING FEELS WRONG
BUT THEY DON'T KNOW WHAT TO DO

(ANOTHER SOLOIST steps forward and takes over.)

   ANOTHER SOLOIST.
WELL, WE'RE HERE TO TELL YOU
THERE'S A WAY TO START AGAIN
FIRST YOU OPEN UP YOUR EYES
THEN YOUR HEART AND MIND AND THEN—

   ALL.
IT'S TIME TO CELEBRATE
TIME TO OPEN UP YOUR EYES
IT'S TIME TO RAISE YOUR VOICE
TIME TO SING IT TO THE SKIES
IT'S A HAPPY DAY
AND THE FLOWERS ARE IN BLOOM
IF YOU ARE NOT OKAY
WE KNOW YOU WILL BE SOON.

ANGELIC GIRL. Dance break!

(They all do a choreographed dance.)

  ALL.
HEY! IT'S A HAPPY DAY!
HEY! IT'S A HOLIDAY!
HEY! IT'S A HAPPY DAY!
HEY! IT'S A HOLIDAY!
HEY! IT'S A HAPPY DAY!
HEY! IT'S A HOLIDAY!
HEY! IT'S A HAPPY DAY!
HEY! IT'S A HOLIDAY!
HEY!

*(Tableau and applause. Several children bring out a manger set-
up.)*

ANGELIC GIRL. Rejoice! Jubilate! Celebrate because today we tell the story of stories—today we spin the tale of tales—
today we relate the life of L. Ron Hubbard: teacher, author, explorer,
atomic physicist, nautical engineer, choreographer, horticulturist…
and father of Scientology.

(ANOTHER CHILD steps up.)

ANOTHER CHILD. Before we go any further, I'd just like to
remind the people here tonight that "Scientology," "Scientologist,"
"Dianetics," and the name "L. Ron Hubbard" are registered trade-
marks owned exclusively by The Church of Scientology.
ANGELIC GIRL. Thank you. Now let's get on with the
show!

*(Focus shifts to several children fighting about who will be L
RON.)*

1. I want to be L Ron.
2. You were L Ron last year. This time it's my turn.
3. (To 2) You're too big to fit in the manger.

L RON. What about me?

2. What about you?

L RON. Can I be L Ron?

2. No way.

1. I'm going to be L Ron and none of you can stop me.

2. Oh yeah?

1. Yeah!

(1 and 2 start scuffling. The ANGELIC GIRL goes and breaks it up.)

ANGELIC GIRL. Stop it! We all know what a great honor it is to play L Ron: teacher, author, explorer, atomic physicist, nautical engineer, choreographer, horticulturist, father of Scientology. But you must not fight. As L Ron said: *(She delivers it straight out to the audience.)* "Ideas and not battles mark the forward progress of mankind." *(Pointing to L RON.)* He will be L Ron.

(L RON climbs into the manger.)

Scene 2.
"Birth"

(They all form a nativity tableau around L RON in the manger.)

ANGELIC GIRL. Ready?

ALL. *(Joyously)* Yeah!

(The ANGELIC GIRL leads them in a rousing reprise.)

ALL.
HEY, IT'S A HAPPY DAY
HEY, IT'S A HOLIDAY
HEY, IT'S A HAPPY DAY
HEY, IT'S A HOLIDAY.
HEY!

(The song finishes and the ANGELIC GIRL speaks.)

ANGELIC GIRL. L. Ron Hubbard was born on March 13, 1911 to simple hardworking parents in the little farming town of Tilden, Nebraska.

COW. Moo.

CHICKEN. Cockadoodledoo.

ANGELIC GIRL. Billions of years of evolution had climaxed with his birth.

FATHER. *(To L RON.)* Goo goo.

MOTHER. When I look at him, honey, you know what I think?

FATHER. What's that?

MOTHER. I think: this is the climax of a billion years of evolution.

FATHER. You're right honey. He will grow up to be a great man.

MOTHER. Yes, he will.

FATHER. And so he'll need a great name.

MOTHER. Yes, he will. But what?

FATHER. I know. We will call him: L. Ron.

(Pause.)

MOTHER. *(Dubious)* L. Ron?

(Pause.)

FATHER. L. Ron.

Pause.

COW. What does the L stand for?

FATHER. *(With flourish.)* Leader.

Scene 3
"Childhood"

ANGELIC GIRL. Even as a child, it was clear that L Ron had superior intellect.

ANOTHER CHILD. He was always asking questions.

(L RON climbs out of the manger.)

L RON. *(Pointing to cow.)* What's that?
FATHER. That's a cow.
L RON. *(Pointing to chicken.)* What's that?
MOTHER. A chicken.
L RON. What am I?
FATHER. You're a human being.
L RON. What am I made of?
MOTHER. Well—
L RON. Where did I come from?
FATHER. Well—
L RON. Why am I here?
FATHER. Well, Ron, we don't know.
ANGELIC GIRL. Ron was confused. These seemed to him the most important questions of all. He couldn't understand why no one knew the answers.
L RON. I can't understand why no one knows the answers.
ANOTHER CHILD. And so young Ron set off to sail the world, looking for them.

Scene 4

"Travelling the World"

(L RON travels the world in a boat.)

ANGELIC GIRL. First he went to Hawaii.

(Several children in Hawaiian outfits ENTER, leis and all.)

HAWAIIAN CHILD. Aloha.
L RON. Aloha. My name is L Ron Hubbard.
HAWAIIAN CHILD. What does the L stand for?
L RON. It stands for "Looking." I'm looking for the answers to the most important questions of all.
HAWAIIAN CHILD. Oh. Like what?

L RON. Why are we here? Where are we going? How can we be happy?

HAWAIIAN CHILD. We don't really think about those things. We just lie in the sun all day.

L RON. *(Shaking his head.)* There's got to be more to life than that.

ANGELIC GIRL. Next, L Ron went to New York City.

(Several harried New Yorkers with ENTER with cell phones.)

L RON. Excuse me. I'm here to discover what really matters in life.

NEW YORKER. What?

L RON. I said—

NEW YORKER. The only thing that matters is success.

L RON. That can't be right. What about happiness and fulfill- ment?

(The NEW YORKERS shrug and EXIT.)

ANGELIC GIRL. Finally, Ron went to China.

(Several BUDDHIST MONKS ENTER.)

L RON. Hi. I've come to your country to try to find the mean- ing of life.

MONK. The meaning of life cannot be found in this world. In fact, this world does not exist. It is merely an illusion.

L RON. Then how can I be happy?

MONK. Life is suffering. To achieve true happiness, you must accept that your life is an illusion and give up all worldly things.

L RON. Give up worldly things? How would that lead to hap- piness? No, you don't have the answers either.

(The MONK shrugs.)

MONK. Sorry.

(He EXITS.)

Scene 5
"University"

ANGELIC GIRL. Ron returned to the United States. He had traveled the world, but still he hadn't found the answers to the most important questions of all.

(A KID IN A LAB COAT ENTERS, clutching a clipboard.)

KID IN A LAB COAT. And so, he turned to science.
ANGELIC GIRL. Ron began his studies at George Washington University.

(L RON ENTERS the university, where he is greeted by a child in a GEORGE WASHINGTON wig.)

GEORGE WASHINGTON. Welcome to my University, young L Ron.
L RON. Thank you. I'm here to search for the answers to the most important questions of all.
GEORGE WASHINGTON. Is that right? Well, I hope you find them here.
ANGELIC GIRL. L Ron worked hard, and he excelled in physics. Soon he learned to harness the power of the atom.
L RON. *(To GEORGE WASHINGTON.)* Mister Washington, I have learned to harness the power of the atom, and yet my questions are still not answered. How is it that humankind has made such advances in science and yet has not managed to discover the key to happiness?
GEORGE WASHINGTON. I cannot tell a lie…I don't know.

(L RON shrugs sadly.)

L RON. *(To the audience.)* Even our Founding Father doesn't know! *(Pause.)* I've given up on trying to find someone else to give me the answers to life's questions. There are millions of people who go through life lost, confused, and frightened. They're all looking for someone else to give them the answers. But there's no one out there for them. No one. So it's up to me to give them answers. I will be the one to give them hope, to give them the key to happiness, to give them a reason to live!

ANGELIC GIRL. And so, L Ron became a writer.

Scene 6

"Writing"

ANGELIC GIRL. In a series of philosophically complex, deeply moving stories, he explored these difficult issues of life and existence. It wasn't long before he was inspiring millions with thought-provoking classics like:

(Children name the titles of his stories, acting them out as well.)

CHILD. Murder at Pirate Castle!
CHILD. Death's Deputy!
CHILD. The Dangerous Dimension!
CHILD. Typewriter in the Sky!
CHILD. Slaves of Sleep!
ANGELIC GIRL. L Ron's science fiction adventure novels were so successful that Columbia Pictures called. Ron went to Hollywood and started writing movies. He started hanging out with celebrities, and he made a lot of money.

(L RON ENTERS with a young actress on his arm.)

ACTRESS. *(Giggling)* It's amazing how quickly you've become successful.

L RON. It's not so surprising, really. I write stories that ask important questions about the human condition.

ACTRESS. It's true. I had never thought about those things until I picked up one of your books.

L RON. And now I bet your life is much deeper and more fulfilling.

ACTRESS. It is, L Ron. It is. *(Pause.)* I also love the parts with aliens.

(L RON smiles.)

ANGELIC GIRL. Everything was going very well for Ron. He finally felt like he was making a difference.
ANOTHER CHILD. But then, war came.

(There is the sound of an explosion. L RON and the ACTRESS duck for cover. A SOLDIER CHILD ENTERS and salutes.)

SOLDIER CHILD. World War II began. Ron joined the Navy, determined to do his duty for his country.

Scene 7
"War"

*(The CHILDREN enact a pantomime version of a bloody WWII battle, set to some inspiring Glory-style war movie soundtrack.
L RON fights valiantly and gets wounded.
Blackout.)*

Scene 8
"Life Boat"

*(There is the quiet sound of the surf.
L RON sits in a lifeboat in the middle of the Atlantic Ocean. He shares the lifeboat with DONALD, another wounded soldier.
The ANGELIC GIRL stands over them.)*

ANGELIC GIRL. After a bloody battle, Ron was left floating in a lifeboat, in the middle of the vast empty ocean. There was another wounded soldier by his side, and together they waited desperately for help to arrive.
DONALD. Do you think we're going to die?
L RON. No.
DONALD. I think we're going to die.

L RON. Shhh. Someone will find us. *(He turns to face DON-ALD.)* My name's L Ron.

DONALD. I'm Donald. *(Pause, then.)* What does the "L" stand for?

L RON. Live. Which is what we're going to do.

DONALD. I'm scared.

L RON. You know why you're scared? Because you're not thinking rationally. You're letting fear take over. Don't.

DONALD. I can't help it.

L RON. Yes you can, Donald. You underestimate the amazing power of the human mind.

DONALD. Ha! The only power of the human mind is the power to hurt others. I used to believe that people were good, that there were answers to life's questions—but then the war came and I saw the truth.

L RON. War happens because people get angry and scared. Emotions are confusing. People just need someone to lead them.

DONALD. What are you, some kind of guru or something?

L RON. I guess I am in a way. I'm someone searching for answers.

DONALD. Well, maybe you can answer this question: why am I going to die in the middle of the Pacific, thousands of miles away from everyone I love?

L RON. You're not going to die. Why have you given up hope?

DONALD. Because I've seen how awful the world can be. Because I have a very bad feeling about this. There's something about the smell of the sea water—

L RON. What is it about the smell of the sea water?

DONALD. It's—I don't know—I think—*(Suddenly lost in reverie.)* It reminds me of my father's rowboat. He had lots of rules about his rowboat. The most important rule was that I could never take the rowboat out by myself. Well, one time I did anyway. But the current was too strong and I fell out of the boat. I thought I was going to die. My lungs were filling with water, I couldn't breathe—but then my father pulled me out. I hugged him, so tight, because he had saved me. But then he said, you broke the rules. It would've served you right if you died. And then he hit me.

(Long pause.)

L RON. It's all right, Donald. You're not really afraid of the sea water. You're afraid of your memory.

(L RON touches DONALD'S shoulder reassuringly. DONALD pulls away.)

DONALD. Don't touch me!
L RON. You have to let the memory go.
DONALD. What do you know about it, guru-man? Stay away from me. Let me die in peace.
L RON. You're not going to die. You have to believe. *(Pause, then poignantly.)* Why can't you believe?
DONALD. *(Quietly, with deep existential sorrow.)* I don't know.

(Pause.)

L RON. Look!
DONALD. What?
L RON. It's a ship! We're saved!

(A group of Navy men saves them.)

ANGELIC GIRL. And so they were. Ron returned from war a hero.

ONE OF THE NAVY MEN. And he had learned something too.

Scene 9

"The Development of Dianetics"

(RON steps forward and sings.)

RON.
I HAD TRAVELED FAR
I HAD STUDIED HARD
BUT I STILL HAD FAILED TO FIND

THE KEY TO BEING FREE
THE WAY TO BE HAPPY
THE SCIENCE OF THE MIND.

BUT THEN ONE NIGHT IN THE WAR
I FOUND WHAT I WAS LOOKING FOR
I SAW HOW EMOTION CAN MAKE YOU BLIND.
AND I COULD FINALLY SEE
THE KEY TO BEING HAPPY
THE SCIENCE OF THE MIND!

*(There is a flash of light and the music changes. The MIND EN-
TERS: played by two conjoined children in costumes depict-
ing halves of the brain. One plays the REACTIVE MIND; one
plays the ANALYTICAL MIND.)*

REACTIVE & ANALYTICAL.
WE ARE THE MIND
AND YOU HAVE DISCOVERED OUR SCIENCE!
WE'RE MADE OF TWO PARTS
IN A DELICATE ALLIANCE

ANALYTICAL MIND.
THE FIRST PART IS ANALYTICAL
THAT'S THE PART THAT LETS YOU THINK CLEAR

REACTIVE MIND.
THE SECOND PART IS REACTIVE
IT'S FULL OF EMOTIONS LIKE FEAR

ANALYTICAL MIND.
THE REACTIVE MIND
HOLDS ALL YOUR MEMORIES OF PAIN

REACTIVE MIND.
THE REACTIVE MIND
IS WHAT MAKES YOU GO INSANE!

ANALYTICAL MIND.
THE WAY TO SOLVE YOUR PROBLEMS
IS TO REMOVE THAT PART TODAY
SAY, "GET OUT, REACTIVE MIND"
AND SEND IT ON ITS WAY!

(The ANALYTICAL MIND motions to L RON. He nods, understand-
ing.
Suddenly, he and the ANALYTICAL MIND leap on the Reactive
Mind.)

L RON. Take that, Reactive Mind! Take that!
ANALYTICAL. That's right! Throw him out!

(They push the REACTIVE MIND offstage. L RON and the ANA-
LYTICAL MIND give each other a high five. The music begins
again.)

L RON.
THANK YOU ANALYTICAL MIND
YOU HAVE HELPED ME FIND
THE ANSWER I'D BEEN SEARCHING FOR.
THINKING RATIONALLY
IS THE WAY TO BE HAPPY
AND THE KEY TO LEARNING MORE!

(The ANALYTICAL MIND joins in with the song.)

L RON & ANALYTICAL MIND.
NOW THE SUN WILL SHINE
AND WE'LL BE JUST FINE
NOW WE HAVE GOT THE SCIENCE OF THE MIND.
NOW THE SUN WILL SHINE
AND WE'LL BE JUST FINE
NOW WE HAVE GOT THE SCIENCE OF THE MIND.

ANGELIC GIRL. With the help of his analytical mind, Ron
wrote down the new science he had discovered. He called it Dianetics.

L RON. When you're a child, every day is happy. Every smell is good. Every song is beautiful. Every taste is delicious. Then you grow up, and you find that the days aren't happy. Some smells make you angry. Some songs make you cry. Some tastes make you sick. And you think: the world is falling apart. But it's you that's falling apart. As you were growing up, awful things happened. And every time something awful happened, it imprinted itself on your reactive mind. I will call these unconscious memories "engrams." Each engram is tied to a sensation. When you took out your father's rowboat and he hit you, that engram was tied to the smell of the sea water. When your sister broke her toe while dancing to The Hokey Pokey, that engram was tied to the sound of The Hokey Pokey. When your mother passed out, drunk, at the dinner table, that engram was tied to the taste of spaghetti. So whenever you smell the sea water, whenever you hear the Hokey Pokey, whenever you taste spaghetti, it brings back those awful memories. You get angry, you get sad, you get sick. But no matter how angry, no matter how sad, no matter how sick, you can't give up. There is hope, and it has a name: Dianetics!

(Three children ENTER, holding the book Dianetics.)

FIRST READER. Dianetics has changed my life.
SECOND READER. Dianetics has answered all my questions.
THIRD READER. Thank God for Dianetics.
FIRST READER. No: thank L Ron.

(They sing.)

ALL.
NOW THE SUN WILL SHINE
AND WE'LL BE JUST FINE
NOW WE HAVE GOT THE SCIENCE OF THE MIND.
NOW THE SUN WILL SHINE
AND WE'LL BE JUST FINE
NOW WE HAVE GOT THE SCIENCE OF THE MIND.

ANGELIC GIRL. So many people came to L Ron to learn about Dianetics that he formed a Church. He called it: The Church of Scientology.

L RON. For a modest fee, The Church of Scientology will teach you how to identify and cast out your engrams. Once your engrams are gone, you'll be able to remove your reactive mind. You'll operate with your analytical mind only. You'll be able think rationally and objectively about all aspects of your life. There won't be any emotions to stand in the way of your success. Then you will be Clear. Ladies and Gentlemen, don't you want to be Clear?

QUESTIONING CHILD. Mister Hubbard, Mister Hubbard! I have a question.

L RON. What is it?

QUESTIONING CHILD. Aren't emotions what make us human?

L RON. No. Emotions are what make us weak.

QUESTIONING CHILD. But without emotions, we'd all be like robots.

L RON. No. Without emotions, we'd live in peace and harmony.

QUESTIONING CHILD. *(Suddenly convinced.)* You're right.

L RON. Of course I'm right.

QUESTIONING CHILD. I want to be Clear.

L RON. And you can be. You can be.

(L RON turns and smiles broadly at the audience and leads the children in song.)

ALL.
NOW THE SUN WILL SHINE
AND WE'LL BE JUST FINE
NOW WE HAVE GOT THE SCIENCE OF THE MIND.
NOW THE SUN WILL SHINE
AND WE'LL BE JUST FINE
NOW WE HAVE GOT THE SCIENCE OF THE MIND.

ANGELIC GIRL. Now it was time to spread the word throughout the world. First, Ron went to Hawaii.

(The HAWAIIANS ENTER.)

HAWAIIAN CHILD. Aloha.

L RON. Hi. You may remember me: I'm L Ron Hubbard. I'd like to invite you to join the Church of Scientology.

HAWAIIAN CHILD. We don't want to join the Church of Scientology.

L RON. Why not?

HAWAIIAN CHILD. We've read that the Church of Scientology preys on the weak and confused, specifically targeting children, the poor, the depressed, and the addicted—exploiting their loneliness and confusion and subjecting them to mental and physical abuse.

L RON. But it is exactly those people who need our help. And we don't abuse them—we provide the strict structure they need to cast out their reactive minds and think clearly.

HAWAIIAN CHILD. But—

L RON. Don't you want to think clearly?

HAWAIIAN CHILD. I guess we do.

L RON. Of course you do.

HAWAIIAN CHILD. *(Suddenly convinced.)* You're right.

L RON. Of course I'm right.

The HAWAIIAN CHILDREN join the Church.)

ANGELIC GIRL. Next, L Ron went to New York.

The harried NEW YORKERS ENTER with cell phones.)

L RON. I have come to bring you the gift of Scientology.

NEW YORKER. Your Church isn't a gift. You charge exorbitant fees for participation in your programs. Although the first Scientology course costs only fifteen dollars, later courses cost thousands of dollars an hour. In addition to course fees, The Church forces its members to purchase your books and tapes at huge markups. The Church has driven many of its members to financial ruin with these high costs. You say your Church is for everyone, but how can this be true if it's so expensive?

L RON. How much did you pay for your cell phone? Fifty dollars? How much did you pay for your shoes? One hundred dollars? How much do you pay for your apartment? *(Pause)* You pay for all these things, but you won't pay for the gift of knowledge—for the science of the mind?

NEW YORKER. But—
L RON. The gift of Scientology is priceless.
NEW YORKER. *(Suddenly convinced.)* You're right.
L RON. Of course I'm right.

(The NEW YORKERS join the Church.)

ANGELIC GIRL. Finally, L Ron went to China.

(The BUDDHIST MONKS ENTER.)

L RON. Come, join The Church of Scientology.
BUDDHIST MONK. We don't want to join. Your Church forces its members to cut off ties with their families and friends and commit their lives completely to the Church. Then when these members become depressed, the Church prevents them from seeking help from loved ones or mental health professionals. There are a number of well-documented cases of Scientologists committing suicide as the result of the Church's negligence. One Scientologist took his own life after the Church drove him bankrupt and instructed him to not to tell his family. He jumped off a balcony, clutching his last few dollars in his hand.
L RON. Why would you need a family, when you have The Church? Why would you need mental health, when you have Dianetics?
BUDDHIST MONK. Well—
L RON. And what are a few deaths, compared to the millions we have saved?
BUDDHIST MONK. *(Suddenly convinced.)* You're right.
L RON. Of course I'm right.
ALL. You're right! You're right!
L RON. Let's sing!

ALL.
NOW THE SUN WILL SHINE
AND WE'LL BE JUST FINE
NOW WE HAVE GOT THE SCIENCE OF THE MIND.
NOW THE SUN WILL SHINE
AND WE'LL BE JUST FINE
NOW WE HAVE GOT THE SCIENCE OF THE MIND.

(The song ends with a joyous tableau.)

Scene 10
Explanation of Auditing

ANGELIC GIRL. *(Referring to the audience.)* You know, Ron, some of these folks seem at little confused. We've told them a lot about your life and achievements, but we haven't explained just exactly how Scientology works.

L RON. You're right. *(To the audience.)* The main process of Scientology is called auditing. In an auditing session, an auditor uses an e-meter to help a pre-clear to identify his engrams.

ANGELIC GIRL. *(Feigning confusion.)* Auditing? E-meters? I'm confused.

L RON. That's okay: we've prepared a small presentation to explain these important terms—using puppets.

(THREE CHILDREN ENTER with puppets: THE E-METER, THE AUDITOR, and THE PRECLEAR.)

CHILD WITH E-METER. *(Holding up a puppet labeled "E-Meter")* E-meter, short for Electropsychometer. The e-meter is composed of a dial, connected to two electrodes. When the electrodes are held, an electric current is sent rushing through the body, measuring changes in spiritual energy.

PRECLEAR. *(Holding up a puppet labeled "Preclear")* Preclear. An individual who still has his reactive mind and thus is not yet a Clear. The preclear answers questions while holding the electrodes of the e-meter.

AUDITOR. *(Holding up a puppet labeled "Auditor")* Auditor. An auditor asks the questions and monitors the e-meter for evidence of changes in spiritual energy.

L RON. We will demonstrate with actual questions used by the Church of Scientology.

(He gestures to the performers, and they begin their demonstrative puppet show for an audience of other children.)

AUDITOR. Do you smile much?

PRECLEAR. No.

AUDITOR. Are you a slow eater?

PRECLEAR. No.

AUDITOR. Do you often feel upset about the fate of war victims and political refugees?

PRECLEAR. Yes.

AUDITOR. Would you make the necessary actions to kill an animal in order to put it out of pain?

PRECLEAR. No.

AUDITOR. Do children irritate you?

PRECLEAR. *(Pause, then.)* No.

(The needle on the e-meter moves.)

L RON. Aha! On that question, the needle on the e-meter moved. This mean we have located an area of spiritual distress. We have located an engram that involves a negative experience with children.

PRECLEAR. *(Playing dumb.)* I don't know what you're talking about.

L RON. That's because it's deep in your reactive mind. But now that we've identified it, we can remove it through a special form of hypnosis.

AUDITOR. By obeying repeated commands such as "stand up" and "sit down," the pre-clear gradually enters into a trance state. He experiences a floating sensation, and then a feeling of freedom. That's how he knows that he has successfully removed an engram and progressed one step closer to being a Clear.

ANGELIC GIRL. Wow! It seems so simple.

L RON. *(Stepping into the performance.)* It *is* simple. *(To the audience.)* And for just a small fee, this amazing technology is available to anyone, the world over.

(One of the children watching raises her hand.)

ANGELIC GIRL. Looks like we have a question, Ron.

CHILD WITH RAISED HAND. Mister Hubbard, Mister Hubbard: what happens after someone becomes a Clear?

L RON. Once a Scientologist has achieved the level of Clear, he is invited aboard the Sea Org.

ANGELIC GIRL. And what *is* the Sea Org?

L RON. The Sea Org is a mysterious and majestic ship that sails the Mediterranean with me at its helm. It is there that a lucky few are initiated into the highest levels of Scientology, and the mysteries of existence are revealed.

CHILD WITH RAISED HAND. Wow. What kinds of mysteries?

L RON. I can't tell you. They're secrets reserved only for those who make it to the Sea Org.

ANGELIC GIRL. Come on…please tell us.

L RON. All right, since you asked so nicely. Ladies and gentlemen: prepare yourselves to learn the MYSTERIES OF EXISTENCE!

Scene 11

"The Mysteries of Existence"

(The lights change and dramatic space-age music plays. A child dressed like a SPACE ROBOT ENTERS. He holds a card and reads from it.)

ROBOT CHILD. The following is completely secret and absolutely serious: it is the story of the universe, as described in the most sacred literature of the Church of Scientology.

(A child dressed as GALACTIC RULER XENU ENTERS. She also reads from a note card.)

XENU. I am Prince Xenu, evil alien galactic ruler. Seventy-five million years ago, I controlled seventy-six planets, including Earth.

ROBOT CHILD. Xenu had a problem. All of his planets were overpopulated.

XENU. But I had a diabolical solution! I told all the billions of people on my planets to come to my palace for income tax inspections.

(CHILDREN ENTER as XENU'S subjects.)

SUBJECTS. We're here to have our income taxes inspected.

XENU. *(Reading another notecard.)* Diabolical laugh. *(Pause. Confusion.)* Oh. *(Pause. She understands.)* Mwahaha! Instead of inspecting your taxes, I will feed you a special potion to paralyze you.

(The subjects drink the potion and collapse, paralyzed.)

ROBOT CHILD. Then, the evil Xenu stacked the billions of paralyzed bodies around the base of volcanoes.

XENU. When I finished stacking them, I lowered Hydrogen Bombs into the volcanoes. Then I detonated all of the bombs at the same time, and all the people were killed.

(There is the sound of an explosion and the lights change.)

ROBOT CHILD. All at once, 178 billion souls left their bodies.

(The children dance like souls leaving bodies.)

ROBOT CHILD. These souls were called thetans. The thetans flew around for millions of years. Finally they began sticking together and found homes in human bodies.

XENU. Today, each of us is a cluster of ancient thetans, trapped in a human body. L Ron Hubbard was the first human to discover how to free thetans.

L RON. *(Interrupting)* Come on! Give it some feeling!

XENU. L Ron Hubbard was the first...

L RON. Louder! These are the mysteries of existence you're reading!

XENU. L Ron Hubbard was the first human to discover how to free thetans!

ROBOT CHILD. On the great Sea Org, L Ron Hubbard trains the most advanced Scientologists to free their thetans, too. Once freed, they become Operating Thetans with the power to travel outside of their bodies, to heal sickness, and to "think themselves" anywhere they want. This is the actualization of the great potential of the analytical mind, the climax of a billion years of evolution…

L RON. And?!

XENU. …And proof of the incredible power of L Ron Hubbard's teachings!

(Triumphant finish.)

Scene 12

"The Arrest"

(DONALD ENTERS, applauding sarcastically. He wears a very official-looking suit. He is flanked by several lackeys. The music and lighting abruptly change upon his entrance.)

DONALD. *(To L RON.)* What a fascinating story. Is that from one of your novels?

L RON. *(Recognizing him.)* Hello, Donald.

DONALD. You remember me?

L RON. Of course—from the lifeboat.

DONALD. I've been hearing a lot about you these days, Ron. You're quite the celebrity.

L RON. If I am, it is only because I have touched so many lives. *(Pause.)* What have you been up to?

DONALD. I'm now an employee of the Internal Revenue Service. In fact, I'm here on their behalf.

L RON. What seems to be the problem?

DONALD. Well, Ron, I have a list. *(He reads from a legal brief.)* The IRS has decided to strip your "Church of Scientology" of its tax-exempt status. A federal court has ruled that your medical claims are bogus and that your "e-meter auditing" is not legitimate scientific treatment. In fact, there is evidence that these methods actually damage the mental health of those that use them. It is alleged that the high fees you charge for auditing and other church services have generated millions of dollars in profit, which you have laundered through Panamanian dummy corporations and stored in secret Swiss Bank accounts. It is alleged that The Church of Scientology has coerced individuals into joining and remaining

in the organization despite the opposition of their families and loved
ones. Furthermore, there is evidence that individuals aboard your
Sea Org have been submitted to violent and abusive brainwashing
techniques. And lastly, The Church of Scientology has been charged
with aggressively harassing, both legally and physically, individuals
who have criticized it in the press or public arena. *(To his flunkies.)*
Grab him, boys.

*(His lackeys grab L RON. L RON'S supporters back up and watch,
frightened.)*

L RON. Must you betray me with a list?

*(The lights change suddenly to a dark, noirish feel, with accompany-
ing sound cue. DONALD'S LACKEYS seat L RON in a chair,
shining a light in his face.)*

Scene 13
"The Trial"

*(THE ANGELIC GIRL presides as judge over the trial, as DONALD
interrogates L RON.)*

DONALD. How do you plead?
L RON. I am innocent.
DONALD. The State presents the following evidence: ten thou-
sand pages of tax records, bank statements, and court documents.

(One of his lackeys hands a giant pile of paper to the Judge.)

L RON. Those papers are nothing compared to the millions of
lives I have saved.
DONALD. Do you deny that your organization grosses millions of dollars a year?
L RON. It is as you say.
DONALD. Do you deny that you made the following state-
ment, in the May 1980 issue of Reader's Digest: "If a man really
wants to make a million dollars, the best way would be to start his
own religion"?

L RON. It is as you say.

DONALD. Do you deny that the "L" in your name stands for "Liar"?!

L RON. No. It stands for Lafayette.

DONALD. Really?

L RON. Yeah.

DONALD. That's a stupid name. *(To the ANGELIC GIRL.)* The State rests.

L RON. *(To the JUDGE.)* I would like to call witnesses in my support.

(The ANGELIC GIRL nods affirmatively.)

L RON. My first witness, ladies and gentlemen, is John Travolta.

(JOHN TRAVOLTA ENTERS.)

JOHN TRAVOLTA. Hi there, Ron. Hello ladies and gentlemen. I'm John Travolta. As you know, I have been a successful actor for over twenty years and Scientology has played a major role in that success. As a Scientologist, I have the tools to handle life's problems. Ladies and Gentlemen, I would say that Scientology has put me into the big time.

L RON. Thank you, John.

JOHN TRAVOLTA. No problem.

(He EXITS.)

L RON. Next, I would like to call Kirstie Alley.

KIRSTIE ALLEY. Good evening. Ladies and gentlemen, I owe a great debt to Ron. By practicing Scientology, I have gained the courage I needed to conquer my drug addiction, enabling me to star in the fine television series Fat Actress…and to promote the quality products of weight loss expert Jenny Craig.

L RON. Thank you, Kirstie.

KIRSTIE. My pleasure, Ron.

(She EXITS.)

L RON. For my third witness, I call Tom Cruise.

(TOM CRUISE ENTERS.)

TOM CRUISE. Hi. I'm Tom Cruise.

*(He flashes a smile. The crowd goes wild. He holds up a brown-
haired handpuppet.)*

TOM CRUISE. This is my beautiful wife Katie Holmes. *(He
speak for the KATIE puppet.)* "Hi everyone. I love Tom sooo much."
(He holds up another hand puppet that looks like a baby.) This is our
daughter Suri. See? She's real. I swear. I swear.

*(His desperate conviction is a little disconcerting. L RON smiles
and motions for him to finish.)*

L RON. Thank you, Tom.

(TOM CRUISE bows and EXITS.)

L RON. Ladies and gentlemen, I have one more witness to call.
Her name is Annie, and she's not a celebrity. At least not yet. Annie is an aspiring actress who showed up at one of our Los Angeles
centers just last week. When she came to us, she was lost, she was
scared, she was looking for answers. Scientology gave her hope.
Annie?

(ANNIE ENTERS. The lights change—things are getting strange.)

L RON. Tell the people your story.

*(Music starts. Go to spot light on ANNIE.
ANNIE opens her mouth to sing…but the voice is not hers. It is, in
fact, the voice of the actor playing L RON. She lip-synchs, as if
the words were coming from her own lips.)*

ANNIE.
DO YOU RECOGNIZE THIS FACE?
THIS IS ANYONE'S FACE
THIS IS THE FACE OF PEOPLE WHO STRUGGLE AND SUFFER

WHEN I CAME TO THIS CITY
I WAS YOUNG I WAS HAPPY
I HAD DREAMS AND I THOUGHT WHAT MADE ME HURT
MADE ME TOUGHER

I HAD NO JOB AND I HAD NO MONEY
SOMETIMES I SLEPT IN AN ALLEYWAY
I STOLE SOME FOOD ONE TIME CAUSE I WAS SO
     HUNGRY
I WISH I DIDN'T REMEMBER THAT DAY.
BUT I REMEMBER HOW I CRIED TIL MY EYES WERE
     RED
AND I REMEMBER HOW I WISHED THAT I WAS DEAD
I NEEDED HELP BUT NO ONE KNEW ME
I REACHED OUT BUT THEY LOOKED RIGHT THROUGH
ME

THEN I FOUND YOU
AND YOU HELD ME NEAR
YOUR WORDS WERE LIKE RAINDROPS
WASHING ME CLEAN
MAKING ME CLEAR.

AND I SAID
RAIN RAIN RAIN
DOWN UPON ME YOUR MERCY
UNTIL PAIN PAIN PAIN
IS A MEMORY
I WILL DO DO DO
ANYTHING THAT YOU TELL ME
CAUSE IT'S YOU YOU YOU
WHO CAN SET ME FREE.

RAIN RAIN RAIN
DOWN UPON ME YOUR MERCY
UNTIL PAIN PAIN PAIN
IS A MEMORY
I WILL DO DO DO
ANYTHING THAT YOU TELL ME
CAUSE IT'S YOU YOU YOU
WHO CAN SET ME FREE.

*(As the song nears its conclusion, we realize that the voice is no
longer recorded, but live. The lights change, and we see that L
RON is singing. It was his voice on the recording—and he is
singing live now. The effect should be an eerie realization that
the words she was singing have, throughout, been his own.
The song ends and L RON turns to face DONALD.)*

L RON. Now Donald, I have some questions for you.
DONALD. For me?
L RON. That's right.

*(The ANGELIC GIRL takes DONALD and places him in the chair.
DONALD looks frightened—suddenly he has lost control of the
situation.)*

L RON. Do you smile much?
DONALD. What kind of question is that?
L RON. Answer me. Do you smile much?
DONALD. No.
L RON. Are you a slow eater?
DONALD. No.
L RON. Does emotional music have an effect on you?
DONALD. No.
L RON. Does talking in front of people make you nervous?
DONALD. No.
L RON. Do you sometimes wonder if anyone really cares about
you?
DONALD. No.
L RON. When hearing a lecturer, do you sometimes experience
the idea that the speaker is referring entirely to you?

DONALD. No. *(Pause.)* I don't know.

L RON. Do you make thoughtless remarks or accusations which later you regret?

DONALD. Sometimes.

L RON. Do you ever get a "dreamlike" feeling toward life when it all seems unreal?

DONALD. Maybe.

L RON. Do you have spells of being sad and depressed for no apparent reason?

DONALD. Yes.

L RON. Do you often sit and think about death, sickness, pain and sorrow?

DONALD. Yes I do.

L RON. Is your life a constant struggle for survival?

DONALD. *(Breaking down.)* Yes! Yes!

L RON. *(Cradling DONALD's head in his arms.)* You are confused by your reactive mind!

DONALD. You're right! You're right!

L RON. Do you want to be Clear?

DONALD. Yes! Yes!

L RON. We will make you Clear! Bring me the e-meter.

(One of the children brings him the e-meter. He has DONALD hold each of its ends.)

L RON. Now is the time to recall your engrams—and cast them out! Cast out the memories of your father!

DONALD & OTHERS. Yes!

L RON. Cast out the memories of the rowboat!

DONALD & OTHERS. Yes!

L RON. Cast out the memories of suffering!

DONALD & OTHERS. Yes!

L RON. Stand up!

(They do.)

L RON. Sit down!

(They do.)

L RON. Stand up!

(They do.)
L RON. Sit down!

(They do.)

L RON. Stand up!

(They do.)

L RON. Sit down!

(They do.)

L RON. Stand up!

(They do. DONALD'S body jolts as if he's receiving an electric shock. He drops the e-meter. All turn and look at him. He stares straight ahead, his face blank.)

ANGELIC GIRL. What happened?
DONALD. I feel like I'm floating. I…I remember nothing.
L RON. Your mind is now Clear.
DONALD. I don't remember who I am.

(L RON smiles.)

L RON. You are a Scientologist.
DONALD. I am a Scientologist.
ALL. We are Scientologists.
L RON. Sing!

ALL.
RAIN RAIN RAIN
DOWN UPON ME YOUR MERCY
UNTIL PAIN PAIN PAIN

IS A MEMORY
I WILL DO DO DO
ANYTHING THAT YOU TELL ME
CAUSE IT'S YOU YOU YOU
WHO CAN SET ME FREE.

    L RON. *(To the audience.)* Now we have given you the gift of
Scientology, it's time to bring our message out into the world. *(To
the kids.)* Follow me!

*(They all EXIT. All but DONALD, who stands alone, looking at the
audience. He sings.)*

    DONALD.
THE SNOW IS FALLING
ON THIS HOLY WINTER NIGHT
AND FOR THE FIRST TIME
EVERYTHING FEELS RIGHT

THIS LIFE IS SUFFERING
FILLED WITH DOUBT AND FILLED WITH FEAR
JUST DON'T ASK QUESTIONS
AND EVERYTHING IS CLEAR.

IT'S TIME TO CELEBRATE
NOW WE'VE OPENED UP YOUR EYES
IT'S TIME TO SPREAD THE WORD
TO THE WORLD THAT LIES OUTSIDE.

*(As the song swells towards its conclusion, DONALD runs to the
backdrop. He gestures with his hands and it magically disap-
pears up into the flies.*
*Behind it, bathed in a strange hazy light, are the children. They stare
blank-eyed at the audience as snow whips around them. The
sound of their recorded voices loops, layers, and distorts until
it sounds like the voices of a thousand identical children. The
sound fades. Blackout.)*

END OF PLAY

PROPS

Cow nose
Chicken nose
Manger
Boat
Cell phones
Clipboard
Lifeboat
Puppets representing The E-meter, The Auditor, and the Preclear
Note cards
Pile of papers

COSTUMES

White robes or other matching costumes all for the children
Angel wings and halo
Hawaiian leis
Buddhist monk robe
Lab coat
George Washington wig
Brain costumes (in two halves: The Analytical Mind and the
    Reactive Mind)
Robot costume
Xenu costume
Suit for Donald in Scene 12
Costume pieces for Kirstie Alley, John Travolta, and Tom Cruise

SETS

Designers have a great degree of freedom when it comes to creating a set for the show. Various productions of Scientology Pageant have used sets that look like everything from futuristic moonscapes to church basements to elementary school classrooms. Whatever set you choose, it should create a fun, dynamic (and bizarre) playing space for the young actors.

Also by
Kyle Jarrow...

Gorilla Man

Please visit our website **samuelfrench.com** for complete
descriptions and licensing information.

OTHER TITLES AVAILABLE FROM SAMUEL FRENCH

GORILLA MAN

Book, Music and Lyrics by Kyle Jarrow

3m, 2f, 2 either m. or f. / Simple Unit Set

Puberty is hard enough without the insatiable thirst for blood! Waking one morning to find thick fur growing on the backs of his hands, young Billy discovers the awful truth his mother has been hiding from him for fourteen years: he's destined to grow up into a murderous monster. Cast from his home, he sets out on a journey to find his father, the legendary Gorilla Man. Combining a variety influences including horror films, picaresque tales, and glam rock, *GORILLA MAN* is a strikingly original new musical. It's a pulse-pounding mix of comedy, concert, and carnival that explores philosophical issues of identity, ethics, and free will. It's a darkly comic coming-of-age tale filled with bombastic pop songs and peopled with lonely freaks by Obie Award winning playwright/composer Kyle Jarrow.

"[*Gorilla Man*] is big, bloody, ridiculous theatricality... There's a
unity of vision and insanity that's exciting."
–*The New York Sun*

"Kyle Jarrow's philosophical fable has an antic charm!"
– *Variety*

"This is a rock musical, and, dare I say it, a great one at that!"
– *Curtain Up*

"Kyle Jarrow is New York's hipster playwright."
– *The New York Times*

SAMUELFRENCH.COM

OTHER TITLES AVAILABLE FROM SAMUEL FRENCH

JUDY'S SCARY LITTLE CHRISTMAS

Book by David Church and Jim Webber
Music and Lyrics by Joe Patrick Ward

Holiday Musical Comedy / 7m, 6f / Simple Set

Judy Garland is primed for her biggest comeback ever - the dazzling star of her own TV special, broadcast live on Christmas Eve, 1959. Judy's guests include Bing Crosby (making some holiday "grog"), Ethel Merman (plugging her Hawaiian album), and Liberace (with a handsome sailor in tow). However, mysterious snafus behind the scenes and cameo appearances by commie-baiting Vice President Richard Nixon (who performs a magic act) and blacklisted writer, Lillian Hellman, (who's forced to read "Children's Letter to Santa" with a puppet) throw Judy's program off course. The surprises climax when the arrival of Joan Crawford is interrupted by the spectral figure of...Death. The evening takes a detour into the twilight zone as the celebrities are forced to confront the lies behind their legends. Devastated and alone, Judy meets a special fan who ultimately proves that, despite her flaws, her shining legacy still endures.

"Magical! A side-splitting musical parody...wickedly funny!"
– *Los Angeles Times*

"Fascinating, hilarious and wildly entertaining!"
– Gerard Alessandrini, Creator of Forbidden Broadway

"Wonderfully strange...a true holiday treat!"
– *Hollywood Reporter*

"A non-stop hoot!"
– *Back Stage West*

"Hilarious! A surreal snow globe highball; a Hollywood Christmas card from beyond the grave!"
– *Portland Mercury*

SAMUELFRENCH.COM

OTHER TITLES AVAILABLE FROM SAMUEL FRENCH

GUTENBERG! THE MUSICAL!

Scott Brown and Anthony King

Musical Comedy / 2m

In this two-man musical spoof, a pair of aspiring playwrights perform a backers' audition for their new project - a big, splashy musical about printing press inventor Johann Gutenberg. With an unending supply of enthusiasm, Bud and Doug sing all the songs and play all the parts in their crass historical epic, with the hope that one of the producers in attendance will give them a Broadway contract – fulfilling their ill-advised dreams.

Gutenberg! The Musical! was nominated for the 2007 Lucille Lortel Award for Outstanding Musical and the 2007 Outer Critics Circle Award for Outstanding New Off-Broadway Musical; and its authors were nominated fro the 2007 Drama Desk Award for Outstanding Book of a Musical.

"A smashing success!"
–The New York Times

"Brilliantly realized and side-splitting!"
– New York Magazine

"There are lots of genuine laughs in *GUTENBERG!*"
– New York Post

SAMUELFRENCH.COM

OTHER TITLES AVAILABLE FROM SAMUEL FRENCH

ADDING MACHINE: A MUSICAL

Composed by Joshua Scmidt
Libretto by Jason Loewith and Joshua Schmidt
based on the Play *The Adding Machine* by Elmer Rice

3m, 2f and SATB chorus / Comedy / Unit Set

WINNER!
2008 Lucille Lortel Award - Outstanding Musical

WINNER!
**2008 Outer Critics Circle Award - Outstanding New Off-Broadway
Musical and Outstanding New Score**

Darkly comic and heartbreakingly beautiful, *Adding Machine,* a musical adaptation of Elmer Rice's incendiary 1923 play, tells the story of Mr. Zero, who after 25 years of service to his company is replaced by a mechanical adding machine. In a vengeful rage, he murders his boss. An eclectic score gives passionate and memorable voice to this stylish and stylized show, which follows Zero's journey to the afterlife in the Elysian Fields where he is met with one last chance for romance and redemption.

"Exciting and adventurous!"
– *New York Post*

"**** THE BEST NEW MUSICAL of 2008!"
– *Time Out New York*

"A BRILLIANT MUSICAL! A superb libretto by Loewith and Schmidt and music that gets under your skin and stays there."
– *New York Times,* Critics Pick

"A MARVEL! Joshua Schmidt's music sneaks up on us until we are begging for more! Adding Machine dazzles!"
– *Bloomberg.com*

SAMUELFRENCH.COM